Robinson Crusoe

Retold by
Angela Wilkes
Adapted by Gill Harvey

Illustrated by
Peter Dennis

Reading Consultant: Alison Kelly
University of Surrey Roehampton

Contents

Chapter 1

Shipwreck!

Long ago, there lived a boy called
Robinson Crusoe. He wasn't at
all interested in school, or books.
All he could think about was being
a sailor.

As soon as he was old enough, he set off on his travels. A few years later, some of his friends planned a trip to Africa.

"I'd love to come with you!" Crusoe told them. Soon after that, the men set sail.

All went well until a storm blew up. Huge waves crashed into the masts and ripped the sails. Then there was a sickening crunch.

"We've hit a sandbank!" cried one of the men. They were forced to abandon ship.

But the storm was too much for their little boat. It was tossed around in the heaving sea. Then, suddenly, a gigantic wave tipped it right over.

Robinson Crusoe felt himself sinking. Desperately, he began to swim for the shore.

After battling through the waves, he reached land. When at last he'd got his breath back, he emptied his pockets.

He had a knife, his pipe and some tobacco. That was it. How ever was he going to survive?

Chapter 2

The island home

The next day, when the storm had died down, Crusoe looked for his friends. All he could find were shoes and a hat. He was totally alone. "What will I do?" he wondered.

He decided to see what he could find on the ship. It was easy to reach, now the water was calm. He found a rope hanging down and hauled himself aboard.

Mmm... Tastes good!

He was so hungry, he headed straight for the storeroom. To his delight, the food was still dry.

9

"I know!" he thought. "I'll make a raft to carry things back to shore."

First, he tied four poles together. With pieces of wood fixed across them, the raft was strong enough to stand on.

Crusoe found lots of useful things
on the wrecked ship: chests of food,
barrels of rum, gunpowder and
guns. He loaded up the raft with as
much as it would hold and paddled
back to the beach.

Crusoe sailed to and fro on his raft, rescuing tools, clothes, plenty of wood and some sails.

On one trip, he heard a strange noise. Was it a bark? He looked around the ship. Suddenly, the ship's dog bounded up to him, followed by the two ship's cats.

Crusoe was delighted. He wasn't completely alone after all.

Soon, Crusoe had enough things to make a home. He found a sheltered spot by a cliff, looking out to sea.

Using the ship's sails, he built a tent. Then he built a bigger tent over the top of it, to protect it from the rain.

At the back of the tent, there was a sandy cave.

"If I made the cave bigger, I could use it as a storeroom," Crusoe thought. But he didn't have a shovel...

"I'll make one out of wood!" he decided.

He dug out some earth and sand.
Soon, the cave was much bigger.
Pleased with his wooden spade, he
made shelves, a table and a chair.

Chapter 3

A new way of life

Crusoe soon got used to life on
the island. Every morning, he went
hunting with his dog. He shot birds
and wild goats for food.

Sometimes, he clambered over the cliffs, looking for birds' eggs to cook for breakfast.

Now I can make bread!

One day, while he was out exploring, he made an exciting discovery: ripe ears of corn. He picked them and kept the grain to sow in the spring.

Every lunchtime, he went home
and cooked his
food over a fire.

He skinned
the animals he
shot, and dried
their skins to use
later.

The afternoons
were very hot,
much too hot to
work. So, after
lunch, Crusoe
climbed into
a hammock
he'd made
and snoozed.

Zzzzzzz...

After his nap, Crusoe stayed near his tent, making things. When it got dark, he wrote a diary by candlelight.

Time passed quickly. So he wouldn't lose track of it, he made notches on a pole, one notch every day and a bigger notch on Sundays.

I came on shore here on the 30th September 1659

Ah! Must be Monday.

19

Crusoe explored every part of the island. There was a beautiful valley in the middle, where orange trees grew...

...and lots of wonderful vines, with rich crops of grapes. It was a paradise.

The juice from these will be delicious.

Say, "Robinson Crusoe".

Robin! Robin!

Crusoe began to make friends with the animals, too. He spent hours teaching a young parrot to speak.

There, there. Easy does it.

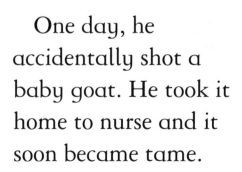

One day, he accidentally shot a baby goat. He took it home to nurse and it soon became tame.

21

Just before the rains came, he planted his grains of corn. The corn grew fast and soon he had a fine cornfield.

But there was a problem. Most of the birds thought the corn looked good, too.

Crusoe had to fire his gun into the air, to scare them away.

Crusoe wondered what he should store the corn in. Finally, he decided to make some clay pots.

It wasn't easy. His first pots had very wobbly edges. But Crusoe soon got better at making them. He left the pots to dry in the sun and then baked them in a fire.

Finally, the corn was ready to bake. First, Crusoe ground it into flour. Then he mixed it with water.

Look at that... Perfect!

He shaped the mixture into loaves and cooked them on a tile over a fire of hot ashes.

Chapter 4

Stuck forever?

One morning, Crusoe walked to a different part of the island. Looking out to sea he saw land, far away. Suddenly, he felt very alone.

25

"I'll escape!" he decided. "I'll make myself a boat and escape."

So he cut down a big tree and chopped off all the branches. Then he began to hollow out the trunk.

After weeks of hard work, the boat was finished. Crusoe looked at it thoughtfully. It was huge.

When he tried to push the heavy boat down to the sea, it wouldn't budge. He shoved... and he heaved... It was no good.

"I'll have to dig a canal from the boat," he realized. "Then I can float it to the water."

But that didn't work either. It was too much for one man to do. "I'm stuck," thought Crusoe sadly.

He sighed. He'd been on the island for four long years and his clothes were in rags.

"If I'm going to stay, I'd better make myself some new clothes," he said.

Taking pieces of goatskin, he sewed himself a new pair of breeches, a jacket and a hat.

Proudly, he tried them on. His new clothes probably looked odd, but Crusoe was delighted.

To complete his new outfit, he made an umbrella out of sticks and covered it with goatskin.

Now, he stayed dry when it rained. The umbrella protected him from the fierce sun as well.

"I think I'll build another home," Crusoe decided. "A lovely summer house in the valley where the orange trees grow."

So he built a tent in the valley and planted trees around it. It was a perfect place to relax in the hot summer months.

One day, Crusoe thought, "Since this island's my home, I ought to get to know it as well as I can. I think I'll explore the coast." And he made another boat.

The second boat was far too small to escape in, but it was ideal for sailing around the island. So off he went.

On his return, he made a map and marked all the places he had discovered. He realized that he didn't mind staying on the island after all.

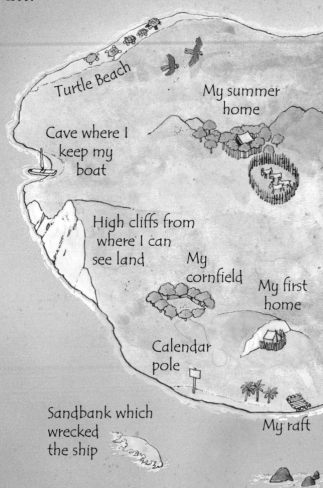

Turtle Beach

My summer home

Cave where I keep my boat

High cliffs from where I can see land

My cornfield

My first home

Calendar pole

Sandbank which wrecked the ship

My raft

"I'm king of the island now!" he said to himself. He had everything he needed and he was perfectly happy. The years flew past.

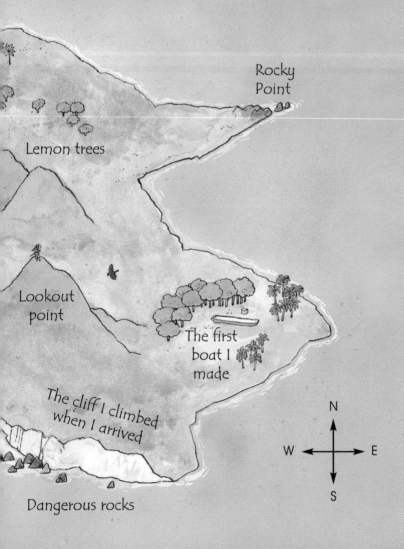

Rocky Point

Lemon trees

Lookout point

The first boat I made

The cliff I climbed when I arrived

N
W — E
S

Dangerous rocks

Chapter 5

Visitors

But then everything changed. One day, Crusoe was wandering along the beach when he saw a footprint. He stared at it for a moment, his heart thumping, then ran home.

Crusoe was so scared, he hid for a week. Finally, he shook himself. "This is silly!" he thought. "It's probably my own footprint!"

So, he went back and measured his foot against the print. But the footprint was larger. It definitely belonged to someone else.

The footprint made Crusoe very nervous. But days, weeks, months passed and no one came... until the afternoon he was out hunting, when he made a grim discovery.

On the beach were the remains of a fire and human bones. Crusoe felt sick. Something terrible had happened here.

He didn't feel happy on the island anymore. Every day, he watched the sea anxiously. Maybe the visitor would come back.

For several months, he waited. Again, nothing happened. Then, early one morning, he spotted a fire on the beach.

He crept closer to watch. From his hiding place, he saw a group of people dancing around a fire and feasting.

Watching them, Crusoe felt uneasy. When their party came to an end, the people jumped into their canoes and paddled away.

Now, Crusoe was very worried. He had the feeling they wouldn't like him to be on the island. "They may find me someday," he said to himself. "I'd better be ready."

So he strengthened the fence around his home and fixed guns into it. Then he planted trees around the fence to hide that. He wasn't taking any chances.

Chapter 6

The captive

Another two years went by, with no sign of the visitors. Then, one summer's day, Crusoe spotted five canoes, packed with people and nearing the beach. He crept closer.

The men landed, built a huge fire and began to roast chunks of meat on it. They had two captives with them.

As Crusoe watched, the men hit one of the captives over the head.

Suddenly, the other captive broke away from the group and started to run. Two of the men chased after him. Crusoe gasped.

The men would kill him. "That captive could be my friend!" Crusoe thought. "I'll try to help."

He followed the men until the main group was out of sight. Then he jumped out and hit one of the pair with his gun.

The other man raised his bow, but Crusoe was too quick for him. He fired his gun and the man fell.

The captive stopped running, and stared. Crusoe smiled to show he was friendly and beckoned to him.

The man smiled back. He followed Crusoe home and they

had a large meal.

After that, the man gave a huge yawn. Soon, he was fast asleep.

The next day, Crusoe tried talking with his new friend. It was difficult, because he didn't speak English. Crusoe started by giving the man an English name.

"I'll call you Friday," he said, "after the day we met."

Friday didn't have any clothes with him, so Crusoe gave him some of his. Friday wasn't sure what to make of them. Crusoe's clothes had a style all of their own.

Crusoe was delighted. Now, he had a friend to hunt and farm with. Friday was happy to share the cooking too.

Crusoe couldn't speak Friday's language, but Friday began to pick up English.

Crusoe was very happy. It was good to have someone to talk to at last.

One day,
they climbed
the cliff and Friday spotted the
mainland. He was very excited.
"That's my home!" he cried. "Let's
make a boat and go there."

"Will your friends like me?"
asked Crusoe.

"Of course!" said
Friday.

Crusoe's huge boat had rotted, so they built a new one and began to gather food for their journey. But before they were ready, disaster struck. Friday saw three canoes sailing to the island.

Help! They're coming back!

He ran to tell Crusoe. Their plans would have to wait...

Chapter 7

Battle

Crusoe and Friday loaded their
guns and hid. As they watched, the
visitors danced around a captive on
the beach. Crusoe raised his gun.
"Fire!" he shouted to Friday.

The men panicked. They fled to their canoes, while Friday kept shooting.

Crusoe ran to the captive, a sailor, and quickly untied him.

The battle was soon over. All
of the visitors escaped, but they left
two canoes behind. Crusoe looked
inside one of them and gasped.

An old man was lying in the
bottom of the boat, tied up.

Crusoe helped the old man out of the boat. As he untied him, Friday shouted with joy.

"It's my father!" he cried.

He rushed up to the old man and hugged him.

Father!

Friday and Crusoe took the captives home. They gave them a good meal and let them rest.

Later, the sailor told Crusoe that his friends were still on the mainland.

Crusoe gave the sailor food and weapons and the man left, agreeing to take Friday's father home.

Chapter 8

Escape at last?

Only a week later, Crusoe saw a
ship moored close to the island...
an English ship! He could hardly
believe it, another ship after so long.

Feeling excited, he fetched his telescope. A small boat was coming  ashore, full of sailors. But three of them had their hands tied.

The sailors took their prisoners to a tree and tied them up. Then they wandered off along the beach.

Friday and Crusoe went down to the beach to see what was going on.

Hello there! Can we help you?

The prisoners stared at Crusoe. Then one of them spoke. "I'm the captain of that ship," he said. "My sailors mutinied."

Some of them rowed us here to abandon us.

"That's terrible!" said Crusoe.
Then he smiled. He'd had an idea.

"Well, we'll help you to escape..."
he began, "...if you promise to take
us to England."

The captain nodded. "Of course,"
he agreed eagerly.

When the sailors came back from exploring the island, they had a shock. Crusoe, Friday and the prisoners jumped out from behind some bushes and seized them. They stood no chance.

"We'll spare your lives if you help us," said Crusoe.

The sailors agreed. They didn't have much choice.

Later that night, the captain rowed out to the ship with the few men he could trust. They crept aboard very quietly... and opened fire.

Aagh! Stop! We'll hand the ship back.

The rebels were taken by surprise.

"Stop! We surrender!" they cried.

The next day, the captain rowed back to shore. "Come aboard!" he told Crusoe. "We leave for England today!"

On board the ship, Crusoe put on his first English clothes for many years. Friday laughed when he saw them.

You look different!

Friday had decided to sail for England too. Crusoe took one last look at the island that had been his home for thirty-five years. Then the sailors hauled in the anchor and the ship set sail.

Friday and Crusoe stayed friends for the rest of their lives. Both loved their life in England but they never forgot their time on the island together.

Try these other books in
Series Two:

Hercules: Hercules was the world's first superhero. But even superheroes have a hard time when faced with twelve impossible tasks.

King Arthur: Arthur is just a boy, until he pulls a sword out of a stone. Suddenly, he is King of England. The trouble is, not everyone wants him on the throne.

The Fairground Ghost: When Jake goes to the fair he wants a really scary ride. But first, he must teach the fairground ghost a trick or two.

Treasure Island: Climb aboard the *Hispaniola*! Cabin boy Jim Hawkins is setting off in search of treasure. But there's mutiny ahead. Jim must outwit cunning pirate Long John Silver if he's to stay alive.

Robinson Crusoe was first published in 1719. The story was based on the real life adventure of Alexander Selkirk, who survived on a desert island, completely alone, for five years.

Series editor: Lesley Sims

Designed by
Katarina Dragoslavić

First published in 2003 by Usborne Publishing Ltd., Usborne House, 83-85 Saffron Hill, London EC1N 8RT, England. www.usborne.com
Copyright © 2003, 1981, Usborne Publishing Ltd.